Taking Back Good-bye

Superstitious Brides #2

A humorous contemporary romance novel by

Susan Ann Wall

TAKING BACK GOOD-BYE

Paperback ISBN-13: 978-1-941852-18-7
eBook ISBN: 978-1-941852-19-4

Cover Images:
  © BENIS | depositphotos.com
  © Oleg Zabielin | depositphotos.com
  © steamroller1 | depositphotos.com
  © Susan Ann Wall
Design Heart of Jupiter Publishing

Edited by Mary Ann Jock

This is a work of fiction. Names, characters, places, and incidents are a creation from the author's imagination or are used fictitiously.

Dedication

In honor of all veterans.

~~

Susan Ann Wall

Chapter 1

"LOOKS LIKE YOU got my sister drunk." Matthew Carson's teasing voice vibrated against her neck, his warm breath starting a sensuous trail that raced down her spine.

Everything Clarissa Dean had done to mentally prepare herself for this moment evaporated like the valley fog after sunrise. She couldn't breathe, couldn't move, couldn't believe her body still reacted like this to that deep voice. Her belly fluttered, her breasts tingled and all the excitement traveled south from there.

Willing her body to behave, Clarissa plastered on her best *I haven't loved you since kindergarten* smile, and prepared to face her first love.

"She was freaking out because you weren't here yet." Clarissa explained as she turned to Matt, who had been absent during his sister's wedding rehearsal and dinner.

Clarissa's breath caught at the sight of him. It had been ten years since they'd seen each other. While he hadn't changed much since they'd said good-bye all those years ago, he had grown up in all the ways a man should.

"As the best friend and maid-of-honor, it was my job to calm her down." Calming the bride-to-be meant getting out the bottle of butterscotch schnapps Clarissa had packed *just in case*. Maddie was now a little tipsy and a lot frisky as she pawed her husband-to-be at a table in the middle of the hotel bar.

Matt smiled, his signature melt your panties smile which had done just that when they were in high school. "Mad-dog was freaking out because she's getting married tomorrow," he said, referring to Madeline by the nickname only he used for her. Everyone else called her Maddie. Since Maddie hadn't yet noticed Matt, maid-of-honor etiquette demanded Clarissa stay put and play nice with the man she'd managed to avoid for over a decade.

"How come you're late?" she asked, her curiosity rivaling that of the cats she cared for at her veterinary clinic every day. "Is everything okay?"

Matt climbed onto the stool next to her, his leg brushing hers as he spun around to the bar. "Yeah, I had some business to take care of."

"Wow, that's not vague at all." Clarissa rolled her eyes and ignored her body's demand for more leg brushing.

"Can I buy you a drink?" Matt asked, tilting his head in that familiar way that always gave her goose bumps.

Shaking off the thrilled-to-see-him chills, Clarissa wiped her sweaty palms on her jeans and tapped the glass she'd been nursing for so long it was warm. Keeping her wits sharp in order to deal with seeing Matt trumped the temptation to deal with the situation by getting drunk. "Open bar. Darren's parents are buying."

"Great." While Matt chatted with the bartender about the best beers on tap, Clarissa turned on the stool. She made like she was watching the crowd, but secretly took him in from the corner of her eye. They were dressed alike, both in jeans and a plaid shirt, though Matt's clothes were tighter, clinging to the muscles he'd developed since joining the Army. His dark blond hair was cut short, the way he'd always worn it even before enlisting, but he hadn't shaved, the stubble giving his sharp jaw a rough edge that made Clarissa's fingers twitch.

When he decided on a micro-brew and got his beer, Matt turned, his legs brushing hers again, making her belly all fluttery. "Here's to old friends," he said, tapping her glass.

He was so casual, so relaxed, just the way he'd always been. Where Maddie could be the high-strung drama queen, her twin brother was the polar opposite. It was one of the things Clarissa had loved about him. Right now, though, it made her insane. How could he act like seeing each other again after so long was no big deal?

"To old friends," she agreed, swallowing her irritation.

He winked before taking a long drink, and even though his innate charm was something else Clarissa had loved, now she hoped his flirting was intentional.

The antique clock behind the bar struck ten. Most of the family had left the party some time ago, leaving only Maddie and Darren's closest friends. Watching the dwindling crowd, Matt and Clarissa sat side by side, not touching, but close enough for that familiar attraction to crackle between them. She tapped her heel on the wooden stool and tried her best to ignore the sizzle. They had never been able to sit in silence without that spark and it wouldn't have bothered her if not for the fact she was pining after a man she couldn't have.

Clarissa had been paying more attention to Matt from the corner of her eye than the rest of the room, but when his relaxed gaze pinched into a scowl, she followed his stare and found Maddie straddling Darren's legs.

"Do we really have to watch the honeymoon?" Matt grumbled and set his beer on the bar before sliding off the stool.

Clarissa grabbed his arm, his forward momentum pulling her off the stool before he stopped. "Leave them alone," she urged, just as she'd had to do at high school dances and parties when Maddie got a little too frisky with her date.

"That's my sister he's pawing," Matt groaned.

"And tomorrow she'll be his wife. Let them be."

"I can't watch this." He finished off his beer and slid the glass across the bar. "Let's blow this party and go somewhere to catch up."

Clarissa held her breath because if she didn't, she'd say yes and all those hours of mentally rehearsing how to say no to him would be wasted. Each time he came home, he tried to see her, but Clarissa had avoided him because saying good-bye again would shatter her already cracked heart. It was hard enough to say no via text message or on the rare occasions when she answered his calls. She always made a point to remind him they'd broken up because their lives went in opposite directions. Saying no to him now, though, with him standing just a breath away, was even more difficult than she'd anticipated.

"I better stay here," she breathed. This weekend was about Maddie, not about Clarissa's enduring feelings for her ex-boyfriend. It wasn't proper maid-of-honor etiquette to ditch the bride-to-be the night before the wedding. Clarissa had responsibilities, an obligation to be there, no matter what and no matter how frisky the bride was getting with her fiancé.

Giving her shoulder a nudge, Matt smirked and raised his brow. "Since when do you follow the rules?"

Clarissa nudged him back, not because she had any reason to but because the innocent gesture sent a rush of desire coursing through her, reminding her of all they had shared when they were together.

"I'm a responsible adult now. That crazy teenager died long ago. May she rest in peace." Clarissa motioned the sign of the cross, something Matt's gram had done when uttering the same phrase and it always made them laugh.

Matt didn't laugh this time. Instead, his blue eyes sparked with the same desire Clarissa had been fighting since first hearing his voice.

"Maybe she needs to be resurrected." There was so much heat in that simple statement Clarissa nearly melted.

No, it had to be wishful thinking. After ten years apart, there was no way Matt still felt … *that* way.

But then, she still felt *that* way about him.

Shaking her head, she forced a laugh, a meager attempt to placate every emotion and impulse wreaking havoc with her heart and regions south. "Most of those rules I broke to get your attention."

Matt leaned in, closing the space between them to mere inches and sucking all the air from the room. Clarissa licked her lips in anticipation of a kiss it would be wise to avoid. There was nowhere to go, though and her body welcomed his invasion of her personal space. "You didn't have to break any rules to get my attention, Riss."

What about now, she wondered, fear keeping the words lodged in her throat as her eyes narrowed in on his mouth. She shouldn't want him like this. Matt had the potential to shatter her heart – again

– because no amount of wanting him could get him to stay. But the way his gaze burned into her, how the nickname only he used felt like a warm caress. It was almost like they'd never said good-bye.

Before anything intelligent filled her brain, or before Matt could deliver the kiss that lingered between them, a loud and very slurred, "Riiiiissssssyyyy," echoed throughout the room.

Matt backed away and Clarissa caught her breath as Maddie sashayed to the bar. Darren followed closely, his cheeks flushed from the little lap dance and make out session he'd just received.

"Matty," she squealed and wrapped her arms around her brother, nearly taking him down as she stumbled. "Matty, Matty, Matty. When did you get here?"

"A few minutes ago. You were too busy playing tonsil hockey with Darren to notice." Matt nodded at Darren before extending his arm to shake the man's hand.

"It's perfectly legit," Maddie slurred, poking her brother in the sternum. "We're getting married tomorrow."

"So I've heard," Matt drawled.

Maddie stood between them, a heavy arm draped across their shoulders. "Aw, my best friend and my twin brother, together again. It's perfect."

Clarissa wanted to point out that they weren't together, but Maddie was drunk enough it didn't matter.

"I'm taking her upstairs to sober her up," Darren said, grabbing his bride and holding her steady.

"I'll take her," Clarissa insisted. "Her gown is spread out on the bed in her room. You can't see it."

"We'll go to my room, order room service since she didn't eat at the rehearsal dinner." Darren gave Matt a quick glance and Matt winked, as if the two of them shared some secret.

"You have her back in her room before midnight. It's bad luck to see the bride on the wedding day," Clarissa instructed.

Matt leaned across her to pat Darren on the shoulder. "Welcome to the family, man. It's not too late to run, you know."

"Matthew Tyler Carson. You take that back," Maddie scolded.

Darren kissed Maddie's temple. "We're all set, babe. I'm not running." Maddie stuck out her tongue at Matt before Darren led her out of the bar.

It didn't escape Clarissa's notice that Matt still leaned across her. She reminded herself to breathe, that he had just been being his polite and charming self to his future brother-in-law and that the lean wasn't intended to be an affectionate gesture toward her.

Then a mischievous smile curved his sexy mouth as his hands moved onto the bar, caging her between his strapping arms. With his body pressed against hers, every inch from breasts to thighs sizzled. Clarissa looked away to keep from bursting into flames.

"The bride's gone and we both know you can't avoid me this trip, Riss. I've got Dad's truck, let's head out to the lake."

Starlight Lake was home to so many memories – love and laughter and tears. It was where they'd shared their first kiss, where they'd made love for the first time when they were sixteen and for the last time before Matt left for basic training. The memory that cut the deepest, though, was when they'd agreed to break up after three years together.

"I don't think that's a good idea," she mumbled, her gaze still fixed on his chest.

"Clarissa," he whispered, his fingers brushing her cheek, as if he was wiping away the trails of countless tears. Fear of falling for him again kicked her heart into high gear. As she breathed through the anguish of having her heart ripped from her chest, she somehow found the strength to meet his gaze.

Clarissa thought she saw her own sadness reflected in his glassy eyes, then a smile curved his lips again and brought back the sparkle. Matt winked before sliding onto the stool, his relaxed charm making her sigh with frustration. It wasn't a good idea to be alone with him, but if he'd only pushed a little harder, she'd have easily given in.

He ordered another beer for each of them, taking a long drink before asking, "How come you aren't married?"

"How come *you're* not?" she retorted, surprised by his off-the-wall question.

"Come on, Riss. You're living your dream. Mad-dog says the Equine Therapy Center and veterinary clinic are doing great. I figured you'd be settled down with three kids, two dogs, and an SUV by now."

She shrugged, pretending it was no big deal her dream wasn't quite complete. "I guess I haven't found the right guy."

Matt grunted.

"What?" she frowned.

"You had the rebound guy, Chris, I think. Then there was the stereotypical bad boy, uh, Bret. Then the nerd, Jake, and the jerk, Jon."

He'd forgotten Joe the sociopath, but otherwise his summary was a little too accurate. "You've been keeping tabs on me?"

"Always, Riss." Those words were a soothing caress, like silk on skin, and Clarissa found herself leaning closer to him, desperate for more. "Mad-dog hated them all, by the way."

"I know," Clarissa sighed. Maddie had taken the break-up as hard as Clarissa had. She'd always called them perfect, her brother and her best friend, and it seemed they had been, but they had also been smart enough to part ways before life made their love imperfect. "You've had your share of girlfriends, too," she murmured. Clarissa had silently listened to all of Maddie's updates on Matt, doing her best to get over him as it seemed he had gotten over her.

He grunted again. "Yeah, but no one like you."

Clarissa shook her head, wondering if she'd heard him right. She dared a glance at him, but he was taking a drink and watching the crowd, offering no indication as to the meaning behind his comment. She didn't *want* to hope. Matt was a soldier. After the wedding, he'd return to Arizona and would probably deploy again soon. As a veterinarian, Clarissa was responsible for all the animals at the Equine Therapy Center she and Maddie and Darren owned here in Lilac Ridge, New Hampshire, as well as the animal clinic which served their small town.

She and Matt lived a world away from each other and certainly weren't moving in any direction that would bring them back together.

Clarissa focused on the water droplets sliding down her glass, the silence echoing between them. This was why she had avoided Matt whenever he came home. It was too hard to be with him knowing they would have to say good-bye again.

She was about to offer up some excuse to leave when Matt nudged her shoulder. "Tell me about the horses."

Of course, a topic she wouldn't avoid. "You know about the horses," she reminded him. Maddie, the center's psychotherapist, loved working with them as much as Clarissa did and would have

7

told her brother, who had been an avid rider when they were kids, all about the center.

"I want you to tell me about them," he urged.

"Aside from Cleo, Sergeant Matty is my favorite," she confessed of the stallion Maddie had purchased on a whim. He wasn't intended to be a therapy horse, but the beautiful horse loved people, even if he could be stubborn at times. Cleo, her horse since she was a teen, would always hold the strings on her heart, much the way Matt did.

"Must be the name that makes him your favorite," Matt chuckled.

"He's charming, smart, handsome. Not at all like you," she chided. Talking Maddie out of naming the horse after her brother had proven futile. She struggled every day with having her twin so far away and often deployed to some of the scariest places in the world. It was hard for Clarissa too. She didn't want the constant reminder in the form of a horse she would work with every day, but that didn't keep her from falling in love with the stallion.

She told Matt about the other four horses at the center, as well as the six rabbits, the four dogs, and the litter of puppies on the way. "We've had several soldiers, working through post-traumatic stress. Being with the horses seems to help, but a few have taken to the dogs. We're looking to hire someone to train the pups as service dogs to provide to area veterans."

"You always wanted to breed dogs. It's great what you're doing, Riss."

The approval in his voice made her heart sing as much as him remembering her childhood dream.

"When are you heading back to Arizona?" she asked, reminding herself why her heart shouldn't be singing.

"Monday," he sighed, sounding like it was a tremendous burden.

"Why so sad? I thought you loved the Army, loved being a medic?"

Matt opened his mouth as though he was going to say something, but quickly closed it. He repeated the drill a couple more times before shaking his head and turning away.

"You're not deploying again, are you?" Clarissa had to blink back the tears at just the thought.

"No. I'm not deploying."

Placing her hand on his shoulder, she gave him a concerned squeeze, ignoring how his body heat engulfed her. "Then what is it?"

Matt turned and took Clarissa's hands in his, clutching them against his heart as he pulled her closer. She was already on the verge of spontaneous combustion. One more affectionate gesture or heated gaze would force the inferno to consume her. "I can't tell you, not until tomorrow."

"I hate secrets," she reminded him.

An amused smile made his eyes glint with mischief. "I know, and you and Maddie can't keep them from each other, which is why I can't say anything."

Clarissa pulled her hands away and stepped back, putting some safe distance between them. "Speaking of Maddie, I should check on her."

Matt grabbed her arm before she could take another step. "Maddie's fine."

She tried to ignore the electricity passing between them, but it awakened everything inside her. "I should call it a night. I have to be up early to get my hair done."

Matt laughed and brushed a hand through her practical but stylish bob cut. There wasn't a whole lot of hair to *get done,* but Maddie had insisted all the bridesmaids partake in all the festivities. "Mad-dog really does enjoy tormenting you, doesn't she?"

"Yes, she does," Clarissa agreed. "She's even making me wear a dress." The dress was beautiful, but way too sexy for Clarissa's tastes. She preferred jeans and cotton, but tomorrow she'd be sewn into a strapless number that showed more skin than it covered.

Matt's hand slid to her nape and lingered as he gave her body a slow perusal. "I hear it's red."

Just like the prom dress she had worn especially for Matt. One thing the twins had in common was their favorite color. Clarissa could only nod because the desire flashing in Matt's eyes rendered her speechless.

"I'll walk you to your room," he said as his hand slid down her arm and his fingers wove into hers.

"That's really not necessary." She ducked her head, suddenly very interested in the scuffs on her cowboy boots.

Susan Ann Wall

"Riss." His other hand cupped her cheek. "Don't run from me. Not tonight."

Chapter 2

CLARISSA BLINKED BACK the pooling tears, still not meeting his gaze as she mumbled a blatant lie. "I'm not running. I'm just tired."

"Come on," he said, giving her a tug and heading out of the bar. "What's your room number?"

"314."

He led her up two flights of wide, mahogany-stained stairs and down a long hall. When they reached her room, Clarissa dug the key card out of her pocket. "I guess I'll see you tomorrow."

Matt held her hand tight, the warmth and electricity continuing to spread from that one innocent connection to the deepest part of her soul.

"Invite me in, Riss," he said, the longing she felt so clear in his voice.

"Matt–"

"Please," he interrupted, cupping her face with his other hand. When his fingers slid around to her nape again, she was a goner.

Clarissa would regret this tomorrow. Her heart would break again when he went back to the Army, but with his breath on her cheek and his thumb massaging that magic spot at the back of her neck, she didn't care about the repercussions.

After three swipes of the card, it finally signaled the lock had opened.

Matt dropped her hand and opened the door, pushing her in. When the door closed behind them, he pulled her against his solid body.

"I've missed you, so much." His lips brushed hers tentatively, almost like he was afraid to touch her, but when her arms went around his neck so she could lift herself closer, he plunged them into a storm of want and need.

Tremors raced through her as Matt pressed her against the wall, a slow burn following in their wake. His touch was gentle yet urgent, as though he were trying to keep his passion caged. As his erection pressed against her stomach, Clarissa lifted her leg, desperate to get closer and wishing their clothes would just disintegrate.

"You're killing me," he groaned against her mouth, lifting her up.

"I need you," she pleaded, wrapping her legs around his waist and arching her back to press against him.

He groaned against her mouth again, grinding against her. "Riss, we need to slow down."

Clarissa wanted to lose herself to his touch, to the love she remembered. It didn't matter that Matt didn't love her now, that this was only one night. He had loved her once and she could cling to those memories as they created new ones from this passion.

Turning, Matt set her on the dresser. He smiled and eased back, crouching to tug off her boots. Her toes curled as he removed her socks.

"Still ticklish," he smirked.

As he stood, Clarissa slid her hands under his shirt, brushing the warm, taut skin beneath his rib cage and eliciting a chuckle from him.

She couldn't hide her smile. "You, too."

Matt stepped closer, filling the space between her legs and kissing her until she wasn't interested in tickling him anymore. With skilled dexterity, he unbuttoned her shirt, sliding it off her shoulders. Clarissa's fingers shook as she worked his buttons.

A quick tug at her hips had her standing again so he could slide her jeans and panties off. In a slow seductive dance, they moved closer and closer to their destination, leaving a trail of clothes until they were naked. When Clarissa's thighs bumped the bed, Matt stopped kissing her. A smile curved his mouth as his gaze warmed her from head to toe and back. "You've grown up," he said, her thighs clenching at the thick gravel in his voice.

"So have you." He was just a boy the last time they'd made love, back when they were eighteen and had to say good-bye. Clarissa cried the whole time, even more so as Matt had held her, his own tears landing on her cheek. The next morning he left for basic training.

Now he was a man, not just more muscular, but bigger. Broad shoulders extended into thick arms, and firm abs gave way to that sexy V thing she'd only ever seen in pictures. It was a good thing she had the bed behind her as leverage because her knees nearly buckled while her whole body quivered.

Matt moved across the room to where he'd kicked off his jeans and plucked a condom from inside his wallet. It only took a few long strides before she felt the heat of his body again. He placed the package in her palm.

Clarissa tore at the wrapper, but her fingers slipped. And slipped again. A third attempt to tear into it sent the thing flying across the room.

Matt followed the trajectory, raising his brow when he glanced back at her.

"I'm nervous," she admitted.

"Me too," he said, his fingers caressing her face. "I know the perfect way to calm our nerves." He kissed her again, his lips soft and gentle, but all the while he held her tight, their bodies burning from chest to thigh.

Easing her onto the bed, Matt braced his body above hers, giving her the perfect opportunity to skim her fingers along his firm chest and abs. The low roll of her name across his lips was a seductive caress that only encouraged her to explore further.

Matt kissed her, his mouth blazing a path from her neck to her breasts where fireworks exploded when he teased her nipples. The slow assault continued as he moved down, down, down until his shoulders nudged her thighs apart.

Then he was kissing her *there*. Her whole body tingled with anticipation and lust, but most of all, with love. Because after all the years and miles between them, she still loved him.

The tingling surged into a storm, the heart of it centered where Matt ravished her. His hands joined the frenzy and she was done, toppling over the edge, calling his name, and nearly bursting from the pleasure.

As she came down from the incredible high, Clarissa thought she might be lost in a dream, that she and Matt had never said good-bye, and her heart had never been shattered. But he was there, his hot skin and warm breath and sensuous mouth leaving no doubt this was real. She caught herself smiling and breathing a happy sigh as Matt slowly and thoroughly kissed his way north, north, north.

"I have to grab the condom," he said, nibbling her ear, but making no attempt to go anywhere.

"Hurry," Clarissa pleaded, desperate to feel him, to love him.

Matt didn't seem in a hurry, though, and Clarissa wouldn't complain about the delicious way he kissed and nipped her neck. He finally pushed away and tore the wrapper open like a man on a mission. As he rolled it on, his eyes never left her.

"Riss," he whispered across her ear as he slid inside her.

Clarissa's heart tested the strength of her rib cage, beating as wildly as it had their first time together – except this was so much more.

They were both sixteen that first time, innocent and curious. They had explored so many ways to share their love, but it had never been this intense. They were no longer kids, nor were they naïve, and had both experienced more than they probably wanted the other to know. Ten years apart should have made them strangers, but being together again was familiar and exciting. Even if it was only one night, it was perfect.

Matt moved slowly, kissing her, looking into her eyes, kissing her some more. He angled his body and explored with one hand as he continued to move in and out, in and out.

She touched his face just to prove he was real, this was real, that they were really making love. "I've missed you, Riss," he said softly. "Always missed you."

Clarissa wanted to tell him she loved him, that she wanted to be with him, but those words were just a dream. In two days, Matt would go back to his life as a soldier and she'd be left to put the pieces of her heart together again. She would fail, because when

Matt left, he'd once again take a chunk of her heart with him.

"Riss," he hissed before an erotic growl vibrated against her skin. He moved with more urgency, his fingers tangled with hers. The storm swirled again, where they were connected. Clarissa squeezed his hands as she cried his name, letting the storm take them over the edge together.

Chapter 3

CLARISSA WOKE THE next morning to the door slamming.

"I'm getting married. I'm getting married," Maddie sang as she came in through the door that joined their rooms. "I'm getting mar…You two did not!"

Matt's laugh echoed against Clarissa's ear as her head rested on his chest.

"You were supposed to get back together, not have raucous sex, on the eve of *my* wedding.

"What makes you think it was raucous?" Matt asked, obviously teasing his sister.

Maddie shrugged and smiled. "Well, my night was raucous, so maybe I'm projecting."

Matt groaned, apparently getting a dose of too much information from his sister. "Why don't you go back the way you came so I can get dressed?"

"You really are naked under there, aren't you?" Maddie questioned, her eyes narrowing with disapproval.

Matt kissed the top of Clarissa's head as he lifted the blankets. "Yeah, we both are."

Stomping back to the other room, Maddie ranted about *her* day and her brother with the naughty DNA ruining it.

Matt kissed Clarissa with the same toe-curling affection he'd shown all night. "I'll see you later."

"See you later," she sighed, a hollow feeling tightening her chest as he eased out of bed. If only they had more time together. Watching him put clothes on made her heart ache. There was so much she should say, but to what end? No words would get him to stay.

After he was gone, Clarissa managed to get wrapped up in a robe before Maddie barreled back in.

"What does this mean? Are you back together? Please tell me you're back together."

Clarissa hated to break Maddie's heart on her wedding day, but there was no avoiding the truth. "Nothing has changed. He's still going back to the Army and I'm still staying here. It was just one night."

"I hate you," Maddie pouted, crossing her arms like a little girl who hadn't gotten her way, "and I hate him. Why'd he have to join the stupid Army, anyway? Everyone he loves is here in Lilac Ridge."

While it was a question Clarissa had asked herself often, she understood Matt's motivation. Her desire to build the therapy center with Maddie was as strong as Matt's desire to serve his country. He had talked about it since they were kids, how he wanted to be just like his uncle who had made the Army his career.

"It's his dream," Clarissa reminded Maddie.

"I know," Maddie sighed. "What about you and Chase?" she asked. They'd only gone out a couple times, but Clarissa was bringing him to the wedding.

Clarissa shook her head. "I told Matt about him. It'd be rude for me to cancel on him at the last minute," she said.

"You little slut," Maddie teased, but the guilt wrapped around Clarissa's heart like a hangman's noose. Inviting Chase to the wedding had been an act of self-preservation to avoid Matt and maybe it would have worked had Chase been at the rehearsal dinner last night. Now, she had to play nice with her date after sleeping with her ex-boyfriend.

"I'm not sleeping with him. Obviously, I have to break things off. I'll do it after."

"After what?" Maddie asked.

"After the reception."

This was a disaster in the making. "Do not bring any drama to my wedding," Maddie warned.

"When have you known me to create drama? That's your job." Clarissa preferred to avoid drama, which is why she hadn't seen Matt since they broke up ten years ago.

Maddie laughed. "Good point. Okay, enough sad stuff. I'm getting married. Get showered so we can grab breakfast and hit the salon."

Three hours later, Clarissa stared at her biggest nemesis. She didn't mind red, as long as it was plaid and flannel. Red satin, specifically in the form of a strapless dress, made her want to catch the express train to anywhere but here.

"Stop scowling at it and put it on," Maddie insisted. "But first, zip me."

Clarissa turned and gasped. Maddie stood in the beaded strapless gown that hugged her curves and flared out at the bottom. "Oh, Maddie. You look like a princess."

Maddie's smile was contagious. "And today I'm marrying the man of my dreams."

"He's going to pass out when you walk down the aisle," Clarissa teased as she eased the zipper up.

"Which I'm never going to do if you don't get your dress on. You know when Matt sees you in it he won't be able to resist you."

Clarissa could argue that she didn't need some little red dress to be irresistible. After all, she'd been wearing flannel last night. The truth of the situation kept the words lodged in her throat. Matt going back to his life in the Army was just too painful to put into words. Plus, her safety net was in place. She'd asked Chase to be her date for the reception as an excuse to steer clear of Matt.

Retreating to the bathroom, she stripped out of her comfy clothes, maneuvered her small breasts into a padded bra, and shimmied into the dress, completing her transformation from cotton-cladded veterinarian to classy maid-of-honor.

When Clarissa stepped out of the bathroom she discovered Matt, not Maddie, waiting for her, dressed in a black tuxedo with a red bow tie and vest. Despite her mouth dropping open, she forgot how to breathe.

"Wow. You look, wow," he stammered. His heated gaze was all the approval Clarissa needed to forget how much she hated wearing a dress.

"What? This old rag?" she joked, smoothing her hands over her hips. "Tomorrow it'll be back in the barn with all the other rags we use to clean the stalls."

Matt crossed the room in long, urgent steps, pulling Clarissa against his solid body. "You'll do no such thing. You are keeping this dress."

She opted not to remind him he was leaving in two days. This was a happy day, the happiest of happy days, and she didn't want to have to fake her way through it.

One hand held her tightly at the small of her back while the other skimmed across her breasts. Matt raised a brow and smiled. "So it is true what they say about making love after midnight. It does make them more voluptuous."

Clarissa laughed while shaking her head. "Don't get excited, it's just an illusion created by a very padded bra. It's the only thing keeping this dress up."

He sidled up to her, nuzzling her neck and sending a flurry of *Oh My God* rushing through her body. "Too late, I'm already excited. You look incredible, but I can't wait to peel this dress off you tonight."

They hadn't talked about a replay and even though she'd be wrecked when he left on Monday, Clarissa hoped for another night with the man she couldn't seem to forget.

"You do realize I'll be out of this dress long before the reception is over," she informed him. She already missed her jeans.

"Shame." His hands skimmed across the top of the dress again. "What can I do to talk you into leaving it on?"

Uh … that. Exactly … that. "What was the question?" she stammered.

"Come on people, this girl is ready to get married," Maddie exclaimed as she came back into the room with her dad.

Maddie beamed and Clarissa prayed it was wedding day happiness, not anything to do with her and Matt, because even though last night had been amazing, they still didn't have a future.

It was a sobering thought.

Maddie hugged them both. "I'm so happy," she gleamed, but

regret pulsed through Clarissa's veins. Letting Matt in opened too many doors to heartache, not just for herself, but for Maddie too.

Grabbing her Dad's hand, Maddie led him to the hall.

"We'll be out in a minute," Clarissa said. She needed to be honest with Matt, now, not later, because she would not be the person who brought drama to her best friend's fairy tale wedding. Matt took a step closer, but Clarissa backed up, holding up her hand to stop his advance.

"Matt, I need you to know…I won't be at the reception alone. I, well, I have a date."

Matt laughed as if she was joking, but when Clarissa didn't laugh, his laughter faded. "You're serious?"

She nodded because any words she might use in her own defense lodged in her throat.

"What the hell, Riss? You bring a date to Mad-dog's wedding knowing I was going to be here?"

That's exactly why she brought a date. As he had proven last night, being alone with him was dangerous. "Yes," she whispered.

Keeping a tight grip on his anger, he took a couple deep breaths before stepping up to her. This time she didn't retreat. "Call him and cancel."

"I can't do that."

"Yes you can, Clarissa. You can do whatever you want. It's a perk of living in a free country."

She didn't miss the bitterness in his voice, but she was bitter too, bitter she'd had to give him up so long ago, bitter that he could stroll back into town and casually pick up where they'd left off before they said good-bye.

"You stupid, stupid boy," she muttered, something she always said to him when they were going out and they'd fight.

"You didn't think I was stupid last night when I had my tongue buried deep inside you."

"No, that was me being stupid," she said, pushing him back to gain a little needed space. "I let you charm me into bed." This was exactly why she'd avoided him all these years. She couldn't be objective, couldn't set her feelings aside to just be casual with him.

Once again, he closed the distance, pressing her against the wall. His cologne reminded her of what they'd shared last night, a surge of desire shooting straight through her. "You didn't let me charm you. You wanted it, wanted me as much as I wanted you."

She couldn't deny it because that'd be a blatant lie. "It was stupid," she reiterated, dropping her head to avoid his gaze and the temptation of his mouth.

Matt lifter her chin, forcing her to look at him. "It wasn't stupid. Avoiding me is stupid. Bringing a date to the wedding is stupid."

Clarissa had a long list of excuses not to cancel and they were all as weak as the one she offered. "I asked him to go weeks ago. It would be rude to cancel at the last minute."

"Then be rude."

"No, Matthew, I won't be rude. I have a life here, a reputation. I'm not going to toss that out the window just because you breeze into town and…"

"And what, Riss?" he whispered against her ear.

"And do that," she said, pushing him back.

Thankfully, Maddie saved the day. "Guys, come on, you can get your freak on after the reception."

Shaking her head as a blush crept up from her chest to the top of her head, Clarissa chuckled while Matt smiled. "Yeah, she did just say that in front of my dad," Matt confirmed.

"We should go before she embarrasses me further," Clarissa suggested.

Chapter 4

CHAMPAGNE SPEWED FROM Clarissa's mouth when Matt walked into the reception with Janie Hollis hanging off his arm.

"Whoa, you okay?" Chase asked, dabbing at his shirt with the cocktail napkin from his rum and coke.

Clarissa cleared her throat, and cleared it again, forcing herself to look away from the smiling faces of the man she couldn't stop thinking about and the woman who was a borderline stalker. "I'm fine. Sorry about that. Oh, God, look at your shirt." She started dabbing with her own napkin, but both their efforts were futile. It looked like he'd gone head to head with a water hose and lost.

Chase grabbed her hand to stop her fussing. "It's fine, really. It's just a shirt."

Pulling her hand away, Clarissa turned back to the door, but Matt and his date weren't there.

"Over at the bar," Chase said, pointing to Clarissa's left.

She looked that way before thinking better of it, swallowing a groan when she found Matt with his arm around Janie.

"That's Matt, right? Maddie's twin?" Chase asked.

"I, uh…"

"It's a small town, Clarissa. I haven't lived here long, but people like to talk. I've heard you two were a thing."

"Were," Clarissa said. "We broke up a long time ago." Since she didn't plan to go out with Chase again, not after falling into bed with Matt last night, she didn't plan to offer him the details of last night.

"Guess you weren't expecting him to bring a date," Chase said.

Understatement, but even if she did expect him to bring a date, she never would have guessed Janie. Before Clarissa was old enough to get a real job, she used to babysit. Janie was five years younger and Clarissa had babysat her for a few years. Now Janie always seemed to date the same men Clarissa had dated. It was creepy, to say the least. Maddie tried to play it off as flattering, that Janie idolized Clarissa, but that didn't change Clarissa's perception.

"Matt's free to do what he wants. Why don't we get some more champagne?" The champagne bar happened to be on the opposite side of the room from the main bar where Janie pawed at Matt in his tuxedo.

"I'm going to hit the bathroom, see if I can make use of the hand dryer."

The DJ announced the arrival of the bride and groom, who had been busy having more pictures taken once the wedding party was released. "Can we have the wedding party line up?"

Clarissa downed her champagne and grabbed another glass. As the maid of honor, she would have to walk in with Brent Daniels, the best man. Brent was nursing a broken heart after his girlfriend left just a week ago for a job in Wyoming. With Clarissa doing everything she could to avoid her own broken heart when Matt left, they made quite the duo.

As Clarissa walked by the bride and groom, Maddie grabbed the full champagne glass from Clarissa. "Thanks, Rissy," she said, taking a long sip before handing it to her groom, who took a short sip.

Drinking wasn't the smartest thing Clarissa could do. She wasn't much of a drinker anyway, and had never been known to drown her sorrows like that. No, she preferred binge watching Monty Python while eating an entire lemon meringue pie whenever the world got her down.

She had nothing to be down about. Matt wasn't hers. Last night was a mistake, a relapse of her good judgment. The fact he brought a date to the wedding proved he wasn't looking for anything permanent. Well, of course, the fact he was still in the Army provided proof enough. That's why they'd broken up all those years ago.

Because Clarissa was the maid of honor, she would be introduced with the best man, Bear Daniels. Matt and bridesmaid Cathlynn Merriweather — AKA Cat — stood in front of them.

"I can't believe you brought Janie Hollis as your date," Clarissa scoffed in Matt's ear.

He peered over his shoulder, a cocky smirk curving his delicious mouth. "Why not? She's cute."

Janie was a borderline stalker. "She goes out with every guy I break up with."

Cat chuckled without turning.

"We haven't gone out in ten years," Matt reminded her.

"That's not the point."

"She idolizes you," Matt added.

"It's creepy," Clarissa countered, a shiver racing down her spine.

"It's cute."

There was that word again. It riled Clarissa a little too much because the thing was, Janie was cute. She was one of those bubbly, always happy, hums when she walks, kind of people. She practically had butterflies flying in an angelic halo around her head. She was like Snow White, kind and sweet, always seeing the best in everyone and everything.

"She told me she's a vet tech at the emergency clinic. She's hoping to work at your practice someday."

She had applied. Clarissa was grateful there were no open positions at the time. She couldn't deal with someone so bubbly, or someone so stalkerish.

"She's great," Jill Butler-Hale, who stood in front of Matt with groomsman Cooper Harris, cut in. Clarissa had been trying to keep her voice low, but it seemed everyone was tuned in to this not-so-private conversation. "She helps at the Barn sometimes. We love her." The Barn was a second chance animal rescue where Clarissa also offered her services. Just one more way for Janie to stalk her.

"You should hire her," Maddie added from behind Clarissa.

"I need another veterinarian, not another tech," Clarissa pointed out. She wanted to spend more time with the horses, but the people and pets of Lilac Ridge depended on her. If not for her practice, everyone would have to go to Sunset Valley. Though it was only the next town over, the people of Lilac Ridge liked to keep their money in town.

"Everyone knows the techs do all the work," Maddie teased.

Clarissa turned around. "The point of this conversation is that Matt brought my own personal stalker to your wedding as his date. The creep factor on that is through the roof."

Maddie laughed — laughed, for crying out loud — making Clarissa wonder when her best friend had abandoned her. Just this morning Maddie was praying Clarissa and Matt were back together.

"What is so funny?" Clarissa demanded.

"Janie isn't Matt's date. He brought her for Chase."

"I knew you couldn't keep a secret," Matt groaned as Clarissa spun around to face him.

"You brought a date for my date?" she asked, a bit bewildered by this whole conversation.

Matt turned and stepped up to her, holding her gaze as he gripped her arms. "Riss," he whispered, but before he could say anything more, the DJ announced bridesmaid Courtney Daniels and groomsman Sean Beckett, the first two to lead the wedding procession. "We aren't finished," Matt said, still holding her gaze.

Hope bubbled up and filled her chest. Matt's proposition to peel the dress off her danced through her mind as desire flashed in his eyes. While her cheeks heated with the flush of that same desire, the corner of Matt's mouth lifted in a knowing smirk.

When Jill and Cooper were introduced, Matt once again said, "We aren't finished," before turning and holding his arm out for Cat.

Clarissa struggled to define the meaning of those words as Matt led Cat into the grand ballroom. Did he want one more night before he left for the army again or was there a deeper meaning to the complex declaration?

"You ready?" Bear asked, holding out his arm as the DJ announced the maid of honor and best man.

She wasn't ready, not for this reception and not for whatever Matt had planned, but she sucked in a deep breath, took Bear's arm, and stepped through the doorway to the applause of all the wedding

Susan Ann Wall
guests.

Chapter 5

AS CLARISSA DANCED with Bear while Matt danced with Cat, she couldn't get Matt's words out of her head. Nor could she reel in the memories of last night and the fantasies they inspired. She needed to get her thoughts under control before they got her into trouble, or opened the door to more heartache.

"Care to swap partners?" Matt asked from behind Clarissa.

She turned to find him and Cat less than an arm's length away, Matt imploring Bear to take the offer.

"Sure, man," Bear said, "as long as Cat is game."

"I'm always game," Cat said, stepping out from Matt's hold. Bear released Clarissa, not even giving her a second glance. If he had, Clarissa might have pleaded with him to keep dancing with her, despite every cell in her body desperate for Matt's touch again.

Matt didn't give Clarissa an opportunity to run. He grabbed her hands and tugged her against him, his body solid and warm even through the layers of his tuxedo.

"What are you up to?" Clarissa asked.

"Shut-up and dance with me," he chuckled.

"Matt," she implored, only to lose the words when he whispered her name against her ear.

He'd always had that kind of calming power over her, from the first time they'd met at Sunday school when they were just four years old.

Along with the calm came a shiver of anticipation and need that raced from where his warm breath passed over her skin to the tips of her toes. Her clenching thighs once again revived the memories of last night, awakening the fantasies she hadn't quite put to rest.

"You smell good," Matt said, "the same as I remember. That memory got me through countless nights overseas and stateside."

He smelled good too, and the same as she remembered. Not cologne, just the mix of shampoo and soap and deodorant…and the man in her arms. He held her possessively at the small of her back, his fingers angled down and dangerously low but not quite obscene, keeping the ripple of awareness wide awake within her.

Angling his head back, Matt studied her for a minute, his gaze searing into her soul, and pushing her heart into overdrive. One hand slid up her back, his fingers grazing the bare skin where the strapless dress ended.

"Let's get out of here. We can go upstairs and I can peel this dress off you, one thread at a time."

"We can't just ditch our dates," she said, giving the room a quick glance but not spotting Chase or Janie.

"We can do whatever we want, Riss."

She shook her head. "I'm not going to ditch my date."

"Then maybe you should stop staring at me every chance you get."

"I'm not," Clarissa huffed.

Matt raised his brow.

"Okay," she conceded, "but it's only because you're staring at me."

"Right, has nothing to do with last night," he drawled.

"Cocky much?" she asked.

"Tell me you're not thinking about it right now, about my hands on you, in you, making you all breathless, begging for more."

"Stop it," she whispered without any resolve. "I'm here with someone and so are you."

"Yeah? You planning to go home with him tonight? You going to let him strip you down and move on top of you? You going to not think about me while your eyes are closed and he's touching you?"

"I'm not going home with him," she affirmed.

"Good, then let's go back to your room. I had champagne sent up, we can order room service."

"Matt," she sighed.

"Come on, Riss. Don't tell me you can't. We both know you want to."

"It's a bad idea."

"It's not. Come on, admit you still have feelings for me."

He must have been drinking because he got that way when he drank. "You're drunk," she said.

"Not even close."

"What about Janie? You invited her here."

"I invited her here to rescue your date so he doesn't feel ditched."

"What?" she demanded.

His cocky grin returned. "I asked Maddie who I could invite here to step in so I could sweep you away without you having any guilt about ditching your date. She suggested Janie."

"So you're using her? Nice, Matthew. Very noble."

"Janie knows exactly what is going on and she was all in, happy to help, even," Matt assured her.

"Why?"

"You can't tell me last night meant nothing to you."

Last night meant everything to her. Matt meant everything to her, but the truth of their situation created a chasm they couldn't cross. "You're leaving," she snarled. "You have no right to ask anything of me."

"I do, because last night meant something to me. Admit it, Riss. Admit you still have feelings for me. I dare you."

It was juvenile, but one thing Clarissa had never outgrown was the challenge of a dare. It wasn't just in Matt's words. The challenge was written all over his smug expression. It pissed her off as much as it aroused her because his words echoed in her head and sent a thrill straight to her heart.

Last night meant something to me. She couldn't deny it, couldn't lie and say it didn't. All she could do was keep her mouth shut, but her heart spurred her on, riding on the coattails of Matt's dare.

She stepped back, frustrated with how aroused she was and how right he was. None of that changed the circumstances though. "Of course I have feelings for you. I wouldn't have slept with you last night if I didn't."

"Riss," Matt murmured, a warning in her name.

"Am I interrupting?" Chase asked from over Clarissa's shoulder. She turned, horrified to find her date standing there, the hurt a little too clear.

She glared at Matt. "You set me up."

He shook his head, biting down on the corner of his lip. She wanted to believe the sincerity she saw there, but this situation was just a little too contrived. She turned back to the man she should have been dancing with instead of going round and round with Matt.

"Chase, I—"

Holding up his hand, Chase shook his head. "I was coming over here to tell you that I'm taking Janie home. Neither of us want to be a third wheel here and it's clear we both are. Take care, Clarissa." He turned and walked away, across the dance floor to where Janie hung her head low, her eyes hooded with regret.

Clarissa turned back to Matt. "I can't believe you just did that."

"All I did was dare you to tell the truth. When he showed up—"

"His name is Chase," Clarissa interrupted.

Matt shook his head. "I don't give a shit what his name is. When I saw him standing there, I tried to warn you, but what difference does it make? You were just using him to avoid me and I'm not letting you do that anymore."

He grabbed her again, much the way he had when this dance started, and dragged Clarissa off the dance floor in the opposite direction Chase had gone.

"We can't leave the reception," Clarissa demanded as Matt lead her to the main corridor outside the ballroom.

"We need to talk," Matt said, leaving no room for argument.

"I'm not sleeping with you again. I can't, Matt, I can't survive you leaving again." Her heart had already started cracking. "I can't." Saying good-bye again would be as painful as it had been last time.

He stopped and turned, his free hand cupping her cheek. "I'm not leaving, Riss. I'm getting out of the Army. I'm coming home, for good."

Chapter 6

"IF YOU ARE playing with me, Matthew Carson, I swear I will…"

"You're hot when you get pissed off," Matt said, his lips brushing hers.

She was putty in his hands when he did that, so Clarissa sucked in a deep breath and dug deep for a little resolve. She took a step back and pinned him with a demand in her gaze.

"I didn't reenlist. I have three months left, but I have two months I can take as terminal leave, so I'll be home in six weeks."

He seemed happy about his newsflash, but it threw Clarissa off balance.

"Why? I…I don't understand." The Army was his dream, why would he give it up, just like that?

Taking her hand, he traced the lines on her palm, pursing his lips and shaking his head. "I've seen so much. Too much. Blood and broken bodies, kids with guns and bombs, families destroyed by war. I don't want to do it anymore."

The pain in his voice was like a dull knife cutting into her. As tears spilled down her cheeks, Clarissa caressed his jaw, unable to find the words to make his pain go away.

"I don't need to fight an endless war halfway around the world to make a difference." Matt stopped the slow caress on her palm and looked at her. She saw pain, regret, but also hope, and she clung to that as he continued. "There's a lot of good I can do here. I have a job lined up, but I'd like to help at the center, especially with the veterans. I can take them riding, maybe train the dogs for you."

Clarissa threw her arms around his neck and kissed him, shock and joy making her whole body shake. "This is what you wouldn't tell me last night!"

Matt's smile stretched all the way to his sparkling eyes. "It nearly killed me not to say anything. Now it's time to tell Mad-dog." He dragged her to the ballroom, straight across the dance floor to the DJ's table where he and Dan the DJ exchanged a few words before Dan turned the music down.

With the microphone in one hand and his other firmly holding hers, Matt addressed the crowd. "Ladies and gentlemen, it's time for me to give my sister her wedding present."

"The only present I want from you is for you to come home, forever," Maddie called across the room.

"Done," Matt said and Clarissa laughed when Maddie's jaw dropped. "I'll be home in six weeks when my current enlistment is done. I missed the rehearsal yesterday because I had an interview at the hospital. I've been offered a job as a paramedic in the emergency department."

Everyone in the room clapped and cheered and Matt released Clarissa's hand as Maddie scuttled across the dance floor and nearly tackled him.

When Maddie finally calmed down and let her twin go, her happiness shined as bright as Clarissa's. "So you two are back together."

It wasn't a question and as her eyes darted back and forth between them, Clarissa held her breath.

"That's something Riss and I need to talk about," Matt said, sliding his fingers between hers again.

Clarissa's heart pounded so violently she thought she might pass out.

"Dance with me," he said again and tugged her hand as Kelly Clarkson's *A Moment Like This* started playing.

"You planned this," Clarissa said, tears still spilling as the song which had once been theirs filled the reception hall.

Matt smiled and pulled her against him. With her head resting against his chest, she felt his heart beating as wildly as hers.

He was coming home – forever. Though Clarissa had often let her mind toss around what-ifs, she never imagined that dream coming true. As she replayed his words in her head, she realized he must still be keeping a secret.

Angling her head back, his warm smile greeted her. "A job interview wouldn't take all evening. You didn't show up until almost ten last night."

His smile twitched. "I spent a few hours with your dad."

"My dad?" she asked, glancing around the room until she found her parents watching from the other side of the dance floor.

When her eyes came back to Matt, his mischievous smile made his eyes sparkle. "It took a while, but I convinced him I'm worthy of his daughter's love. Riss, we may have said good-bye all those years ago, but I never stopped loving you."

His mouth claimed hers. Clarissa melted into him, her arms wrapped so tightly around him they ached. Matt was all she ever wanted and now she was finally going to get to keep him. Forever.

The kiss slowed until his mouth released hers, but he rested his forehead against hers, letting his love touch her with the intensity of his gaze. "I love you," he said, his fingers brushing her cheek. "Tell me there's a chance you can love me again, too."

Clarissa shook her head. "Not again," she admitted. "Still, Matt. I still love you."

She didn't think they could get any closer, but he pulled her hard against his body. "I'm taking back good-bye. I will never again say that to you, Riss. Never."

Chapter 7

THE PAST TWO days had been a whirlwind of emotions, with her first and only love breezing back into her life and her best friend getting married. Clarissa should be exhausted given how little sleep Matt let her get the past two nights — with no complaints from Clarissa, of course — but with her hand in Matt's as they walked through the sleepy streets of Lilac Ridge, adrenaline or something more powerful kept her steps light.

"I never walk through town," Clarissa admitted, her two yellow labs, Vanilla and Maple, leading them on with wagging tales. "I forgot how beautiful it is."

A few trees showed signs of autumn, but green still dominated the leaves, a gentle breeze rustling through them. After passing by the main square, they turned down Church Street, aptly named because it housed the oldest church in town. Picnic tables were scattered on the lawn, now empty, but often occupied after church and during lunch on warm days like this.

Matt led Clarissa to a table nestled amongst the bordering trees, the same table they had shared countless times as children and teens, both after church and whenever they wanted a quiet place just to be together. She sat on the bench, facing out, leaning back on the table while Matt grabbed a couple of sticks from the bushes.

With a commanding voice, he ordered the dogs to sit and they obeyed as if he was their commanding officer. Once Clarissa released the leashes from their collars, Matt tossed the sticks across the church lawn and commanded the two pups to go fetch before taking a seat.

"I missed this. I don't regret a minute I spent in the Army, but no place ever felt like home, not without you."

"I feel like this is all a dream," Clarissa admitted as the dogs returned. "I'm afraid I'll wake up tomorrow and you'll be gone and I won't ever see you again."

Matt took both sticks, once again commanding the dogs to sit before chucking the sticks across the lawn again. When his fingers moved over hers in a gentle caress, her restless heart raced with hope for what their future might hold. "I told you, no more good-byes. I have to go back tomorrow, but it's only temporary. I'll be back here, back in your arms in six weeks."

"Seems too good to be true."

With a gentle squeeze of her hand, Matt smiled. "I promise, it's not. That reminds me of another promise I made to you."

"Oh yeah?" she asked.

The dogs returned, and this time, after Matt took the offered sticks, they both sat, tails brushing against the grass as they waited patiently for their new friend to throw the sticks once more.

"Good dogs," Matt praised, commanding them to wait before throwing the sticks again. Vanilla, still being an undisciplined puppy took off immediately, but Maple, the seasoned veteran, stood her ground, waiting for her command. "Fetch!" Matt ordered, and she was off, joining her sister across the lawn.

Matt stood and pulled something from his pocket. Clarissa had to blink twice to realize what it was.

Holding out the ring, Matt dropped to one knee. "You were my first love, Clarissa, my only love. Please say you'll marry me."

They were just five years old when little Matty Carson got down on one knee and proposed to Clarissa the first time, right in this very spot. He had stolen his grandmother's ring from her jewelry box. Back then, it was too big, but he pulled a string from his pocket and made a necklace for Clarissa to wear it, making her promise she would never take it off. It was a promise she had no intention of breaking.

As soon as her parents saw the diamond dangling over her dress, they made her return it, but Matt whispered, "Don't worry, Rissa, I'll give it to you again someday."

When they were fifteen and Matt asked Clarissa to be his girlfriend, he promised someday he would put his grandmother's ring on her finger, but when they were eighteen and decided it was best to go their separate ways, Clarissa let go of the hope of wearing the beautiful diamond.

Now as Matt balanced on one knee in front of her, all her hopes and dreams rushed back in, the fairy tale she'd played over and over in her mind since the age of five getting a breath of new life.

"Yes, Matt, yes. I will marry you."

Epilogue

IF CLARISSA THOUGHT Maddie's wedding weekend was a whirlwind, it was nothing compared to the last seven weeks. After Matt proposed, he insisted they get married right away, as soon as he returned, and left Clarissa to work out the details. She'd kept it simple, a small ceremony with their family and friends in a quiet park on Starlight Lake with a pot luck reception in the same spot to follow. The foliage was at peak, the colors providing an awe-inspiring backdrop beyond the bright blue waters that reflected the clear blue sky.

Clarissa had thought Matt would wear his Army uniform, but he insisted on a tailored suit instead, saying his chapter in the Army was behind them and he didn't want their wedding day to have a hint of the one thing that had kept them apart for so long.

They had exchanged vows, words they had written together over numerous video calls, speaking of a lifelong love that no amount of time or distance could dispel. They kissed to the applause of their family and friends, Maddie getting a little crazy with her "whoop whoop whoop" and fist pumps. She had stood in as matron of honor, Darren as the best man, and now that the pictures were all done and the party underway, Clarissa took a moment to gaze at her husband, the man she had always loved, the man who had taken back good-bye and promised to love her forever.

"You okay?" he said, turning to her, concern in his eyes.

"I'm still worried I'm going to wake up and find this is all a dream."

Matt took her left hand and placed it over his heart. A solid rhythm thumped beneath muscle and rib cage, warming her own heart and reminding her of the nights they had already shared. Tonight would be their first as husband and wife and Clarissa had no doubt it would be a night she would never forget.

Caressing her hand, specifically the rings he had placed on her finger with his promise of love, Matt pursed his lips and shook his head. His other hand cupped her cheek, his thumb brushing the tears from her cheek. "I love you so much, Riss. I promise to spend every day making you happy — for the rest of our lives. Don't ever doubt that or think it isn't real."

Clarissa nuzzled his warm, rough hand, knowing he meant every word. Even before joining the Army, he had always had a sense of duty, honor, and integrity. He had never lied, never hurt her, and knew he never would

"I love you, Matt," she said, her arms going around his waist and holding him as though her life depended on it. In front of their family and friends, he had promised to love, honor, and cherish her, and Clarissa had promised the same.

Finding the slit in her simple gown, Matt's fingers moved up her thigh and over the garter. He slid a finger beneath it with a groan, the sound vibrating against her temple.

"I love this dress," he murmured, his hand moving a little higher.

"We have an audience," she reminded him, but as they turned toward the festivities, the only two paying them any attention were Vanilla and Maple.

Matt picked up the two sticks sitting at the dogs' feet and tossed them in the water. "Matt, no," Clarissa said, but he just smirked. "Come on Riss, it's time to have a little fun." He turned back to the dogs, Vanilla practically vibrating with anticipation, not unlike Clarissa. "Fetch," he commanded and the two dogs were past them in a second, diving into the water and paddling out to the rocks without a care in the world.

Without missing a beat, Matt grabbed Clarissa, pulling her against his solid body, his hand easing up her thigh again. "Now, my beautiful wife, where were we?"

~　　~

Dear Reader,

I first wrote this as a short story for a second chance anthology. Plans for the anthology imploded and I was left wondering what to do with this wonderful story. I always felt that Clarissa and Matt's journey would be a bridge between two series, The Superstitious Brides and Sunset Valley, so I settled on expanding this story into a novelette with plans to continue their journey in a later novel in the Sunset Valley series. So, if you loved their reunion story, there will be more as they learn how to make their marriage work after so many years apart.

Thank you for being a part of my journey. If you enjoyed this or any of my other books, please leave an honest review at Amazon or your preferred review site so other readers can find these stories.

All the best,

Susan

Continue reading for an excerpt from *Mistletoe Marathon*, the next story in the Superstitious Brides series.

This novella is available November 1, 2016 in the *Spicy Christmas Kisses 2* box set.

Amber James had a plan. So what if it required the planets to align, a virginal sacrifice, and worst of all, running. It was a plan, a solid, almost-infallible plan.

She'd be better off selling her soul to the devil, and she just might since that was Plan B. Plan C — to rework her list of potential perfect husbands — was a last resort if all else failed.

Plan A would work, it had to. With a first win under her belt, all her hard work was falling into place.

"A toast to Amber," Clint Avery, her personal trainer, bellowed, holding up a dark beer and commanding the attention of everyone in the pub. "Today was her third half marathon and she finished first in the women's division."

Cheers echoed throughout Madigan's and Amber gave herself permission to enjoy it. For the first time ever, she wasn't the average girl with average grades, average athletic ability, average looks…

No, today she excelled. She was a winner for the first time in her life, with a trophy and everything, and no one could take that away from her.

"Amber, you worked hard, sister, you deserve this." Pete Mitchell, one of her best friends and the man who had inspired her plan, handed her a beer, an amber ale, his idea of a joke since one, he didn't drink, and two, her name was Amber. The whole sister reference made Amber want to hurl, but she took the offered glass and downed half in one go because, yeah, she did deserve it.

"You better watch out, man," Aiden Black, her other best friend since second grade and boss since five months ago, teased. "At this

Excerpt

rate, she's going to be kicking your ass."

"If she's going to kick my ass, she's going to need a better trainer," Pete chortled.

"Your ass is mine," Clint responded.

"Boys, boys, boys, let's dial back the testosterone. This is supposed to be about Amber," Sadie McAlister added. Sadie worked for billionaire and all around good guy Austin Hale. She'd been in the running group long before Amber joined, claimed it was therapy and kept her from killing her boss. She always said that little bit with a sinister smile. Amber loved Sadie because she was relatively new to town and didn't have to pretend to remember Amber from their childhood. Being average made her pretty forgettable.

"To Amber," Clint repeated, and everyone else chimed in.

Amber finished the rest of the ale and asked for another because a little bit of liquid courage was a good thing. Her plan was to win the Mistletoe Marathon, Lilac Ridge's annual race. It was tradition for the first man and first woman to cross the finish line to share a kiss under the mistletoe. Pete had won the marathon for the last two years and held titles from two previous years, before he had joined the army. Since Amber needed a husband and Pete topped her list of local bachelors who qualified as perfect husband material, her plan was to be the first female to cross the finish line so that Pete would have no choice but to kiss her under the mistletoe. Sparks would fly, passion would take over, marriage would be a natural transition, and her life would come together, wrapped in a pretty red bow.

Clint delivered the next ale. "Don't overdue it, babe. You've got cross-train tomorrow and don't want to do that with a hangover."

"Cross-train? I thought the day after a race was supposed to be a rest day?"

Clint took a long drink of his own beer. "No rest for the wanton," he whispered. Clint, also somewhat new to town and a trusted confidante, knew Amber's plan. He thought she was crazy, but he kept her on task, at least with the training part of her plan. "You still have a marathon to train for, and the clock is ticking. The first weekend in December is only eight weeks away. You need to break the fifteen mile goal next Saturday."

"But—"

"Every week you've had a race, you've lost traction. The races are great for you motivation and mark your progress, but the extra rest day is doing more harm than good. This week, we're going to stick to the schedule, cross-train tomorrow, rest Monday, then back to running Tuesday. She hated running.

Ridiculous, yes, but running was the necessary evil to land the only man within a twenty-mile radius who qualified as perfect husband material.

"Slave driver," she muttered.

Clint laughed. "That's why I get paid the big bucks."

No argument there. Amber could have gone on vacation with all the money she'd spent on training for this marathon. She'd tried to do it on her own with an app on her phone, but she lacked the discipline to stick with it. Clint not only kept her on task, but challenged her to dig deep and do more, work harder, beat her previous goals. She couldn't have won the women's division today without him there to push her.

"I'm heading out, chickie," Sadie said, giving Amber a hug. "I'll see you Tuesday."

Sadie was a runner too, but she preferred the shorter distances. Clint led a running group on Tuesdays and Thursdays. That's how Amber had met Sadie, who had been in the group since moving to Lilac Ridge a year and a half ago.

"Call me if something happens," Sadie whispered, also privy to Amber's plan.

"I'm taking off too," Aiden said. "With any luck, Courtney will be done with school work and still awake."

Clint and Pete patted Aiden on the shoulder, wishing him luck.

"If you two are going to hang around, I'm going to hit the ladies' room," Pete said.

Excerpt

"I'll hang out," Clint drawled, sitting back in his chair.

Pete sauntered off, a slight limp in his gait. He'd lost a leg, just below the knee, while deployed with the army. He'd always been a runner and always fit, but long races took a toll on him now.

Maybe if she could get him alone, she could talk him into heading out, letting her give him a massage. Maybe a massage would lead to more.

"That pretty blonde has been staring at you all night," Amber said to Clint, nodding toward the woman who kept glancing over her shoulder. "You should go chat her up."

"Your subtle attempt to get Pete alone?" he asked.

Someone was always around. At work, it was Aiden, because, well, he owned the winery and Pete and Amber both worked for him. Pete preferred to run alone, but occasionally he joined the running group. With five to eight runners on any given night, she had little chance of alone time with the man, even if she could keep pace with him, which she couldn't. Opportunities like this seldom presented themselves.

"I'm just saying, if I'm the only one left for Pete to drive home…"

"Then maybe he'll drive you all the way home," Clint finished.

"You men and your euphemisms. Go try one on her."

"I'd rather try all my isms on you," he said. "Maybe even a few - asms."

Amber laughed. "It's no wonder you're single with lines like that."

"You love my lines, admit it."

She should tell him to stop flirting because she wasn't any good at it, but Clint put the O in H-O-T and Amber enjoyed the attention because she so rarely got any from men of Clint's caliber.

Looking toward the bathroom, she noticed Pete chatting up a pretty brunette. Great, just what she needed, competition.

"Your subtlety isn't working, Amber. Maybe it's time to up your game."

"I've tried to up my game," she countered, a shiver racing up her spine at the memory of her feeble attempts to get Pete to think of her as something more than his good ole pal, or worse, as a sister. "I've invited him to dinner, invited him kayaking, even tried to share a room with him when we did that breast cancer run in Vermont. He doesn't take me seriously."

"And you think a kiss under the mistletoe is going to change that?"

"Absolutely." The confidence in her voice was a big, fat lie, and based on Clint's expression, he knew it.

"I don't get it. There are plenty of men out there. Why are you trying so hard to impress someone who doesn't return your affection?"

Because Pete was perfect husband material. He had a good job and because Amber was the human resources manager at the winery, she knew exactly how much he made. She wasn't superficial, but a good job and stable salary were important when starting a family, her ultimate goal. Which brought her to the genetic part of the equation. Pete was hot. He was on a different scale from Clint, who had the whole bad-boy vibe going on. Pete didn't just look the nice guy part, he was a nice guy, always had been. He had a great family, too, and he was familiar. There were no unknowns with Pete, no surprises.

When she didn't answer, Clint took her hand, his thumb caressing her knuckles. "Why not go out with me?"

She laughed, a spit your drink kind of laugh, so lucky for her, she hadn't been taking a drink.

"Why is that funny?" he asked.

Amber pulled her hand away because even though she liked the attention, she didn't want to give Clint the wrong idea.

"We're not really in the same league," she admitted. Amber wasn't even in the minor league, or hell, even little league. When it came to men and dating, she was on the biddy team.

"Are you playing on a girl's only team?" he asked, brow raised.

"Of course not," she chuffed. That would be her sister's team.

Excerpt

Amber definitely preferred the co-ed team, not that she played often. She'd mostly been sitting the bench her whole life.

"Then we're in the same league, babe."

They weren't. Clint was gorgeous, experienced, the kind of guy who could have any woman he wanted. He was a shameless flirt and she'd heard Pete tell enough stories to know that Clint's flirting scored him countless home runs.

"You're very sweet and good for my self-esteem." She sat up straight and took a drink when Pete made his way back to the table.

"Guys, this is Sam."

"Hi, Sam," Amber and Clint said in stereo as if they were in a group meeting.

"I hope you don't mind, but I'm going to steal Pete for a while. He promised to buy me a drink."

Amber did mind. She was making strides toward getting Pete to look at her as more than a friend. Sam threatened her progress.

Pete winked and followed Sam across the bar.

"I'm going home," Amber whined.

Clint shook his head. "Don't let that," he waved across the bar, "ruin the celebration. You owned that race today. You should be proud of how far you've come."

"I am," she whispered, but all her hard work would be for nothing if Pete didn't get the message that she was doing all this for him.

~~~

Also Available

PUGET SOUND ~ ALIVE WITH LOVE SERIES
The Sound of Consequence (April 2013)
The Sound of Betrayal (August 2013)
The Sound of Suspicion (January 2014)
The Sound of Deception (June 2014)
The Sound of Circumstance (December 2015)
The Sound of Reluctance (Coming Soon)

FIGHTING BACK FOR LOVE SERIES
Relay For Love (May 2011)
A Flame Burns Inside (January 2012)
Worth the Fight (Coming in Soon)

SUPERSTITIOUS BRIDES SERIES
Marrying for Love (January 2015)
For the Love of Chocolate (February 2015)
3rd Trip to the Altar (August 2016)
The Perfect Pairing (September 2016)
Taking Back Good-bye (November 2016)
Mistletoe Marathon (November 2016)

DEVON TAGGART SUSPENSE
Broken Strings (April 2016)

SUNSET VALLEY WOMEN'S FICTION SERIES
Whisper to a Scream (Coming Soon)

Meet the Author

Big dreamer and certifiable overachiever Susan Ann Wall embraces life at full speed and volume. She's a beer and tea snob, can be bribed with dark chocolate, and the #1 thing on her bucket list is to be the center of a Bon Jovi flash mob.

Susan is a multi-genre author of racy, rule-breaking romance, women's fiction, and erotic fiction (her erotic titles are published as Ann Victor). Her bragging rights include more than 15 books in six different series, three perfect children, adopting two amazing rescue dogs, and a happily ever after that started while serving in the U.S. Army and has spanned two decades (which is crazy since she's not a day over 29).

In her next life, Susan plans to be a 5 foot 10, size 8 rock star married to a chiropractor and will not be terrified of large bridges, spiders, or quiet people (shiver).

Photo by BLC Photography

You can find Susan online at:
www.susanannwall.com
Facebook: Author Susan Ann Wall
Twitter: @susanannwall

www.ingramcontent.com/pod-product-compliance
Lightning Source LLC
Chambersburg PA
CBHW071218130626
46555CB00004B/1752